The Case of the Missing
Sparkle-izer

By Bill Scollon
Illustrated by Loter, Inc.

WWW.ABDOPUBLISHING.COM

Reinforced library bound edition published in 2015 by Spotlight, a division of ABDO
PO Box 398166, Minneapolis, Minnesota 55439. Spotlight produces high-quality reinforced library
bound editions for schools and libraries. Published by agreement with Disney Enterprises, Inc.

Printed in the United States of America, North Mankato, Minnesota.
052014   072014

DISNEP PRESS
New York • Los Angeles

THIS BOOK CONTAINS
RECYCLED MATERIALS

CATALOGING-IN-PUBLICATION DATA

Scollon, Bill.
 Minnie: the case of the missing sparkle-izer / Bill Scollon ; illustrations by Loter, Inc.
  p. cm. -- (World of reading. Level Pre-1)
 Summary: When Minnie's sparkle-izer turns up missing, her nieces, Millie and Melody, search for it.
 1. Minnie Mouse (Fictitious character)--Juvenile fiction. 2. Twins--Juvenile fiction. 3. Dress accessories--
Juvenile fiction. I. Loter, Inc., ill. II. Title. III. Series.
 [E]--dc23

 978-1-61479-248-2 (Reinforced Library Bound Edition)

Spotlight
A Division of ABDO
www.abdopublishing.com

It is a special day at 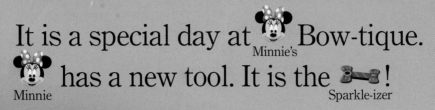 Bow-tique. 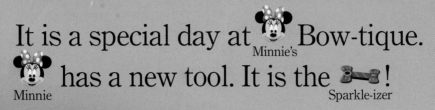 has a new tool. It is the 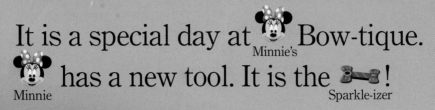!

Minnie's

Minnie

Sparkle-izer

2

"Today," says Minnie , "I'll add free sparkles to any bow."

3

 and  are first.
Millie   Melody

"Hello, Aunt !" they cry.
Minnie

Melody wants pink sparkles on her bow.

Millie wants purple sparkles.

"That will be pretty," says Minnie.

5

Here come Figaro and Bella!
They race across Minnie's table.
"Look out!" Daisy cries.

 and  settle down.
Figaro   Bella

It is time for  to use her .
                Minnie   Sparkle-izer

Oh, no! The  is missing!
              Sparkle-izer

"Where did it go?" asks Minnie.
"It's a mystery," says Melody.
"The mystery of the missing Sparkle-izer!"

"We'll find the  ," say the twins.
<small>Sparkle-izer</small>
 asks the girls to hurry.
<small>Minnie</small>
Everyone is waiting!

 and  look for clues.
Millie   Melody

 sees a trail of  .
Melody   sparkles

"Let's follow the  !"
                   sparkles

The  lead to  clock!
sparkles   Cuckoo-Loca's

"What's up?" says .
Cuckoo-Loca

"Look at her ," says .
bow   Millie

"It ."
sparkles

 used the  on her  .
Cuckoo-Loca   Sparkle-izer   bow

Then she gave it to  .
Clarabelle

"We have to find  !" says  .
Clarabelle   Melody

Bam! Bam! Bam!

"Sounds like a ," says .
hammer   Cuckoo-Loca

"I bet it's !" cries .
Clarabelle   Melody

15

Bam! Bam! Bam!
"It *is* a ," says .
Everyone listens.

hammer

Millie

Bam! Bam! Bam!

"It's coming from in there!" says .
Minnie

The twins and  rush in!
Minnie

🐮 is hanging a 🪞.
Clarabelle   mirror

"The 🪞 has ✨!" says 🐭.
mirror   sparkles   Melody

18

 used the last.
Clarabelle   Sparkle-izer

She left it next to a box of .
bows

"The are here," says.
bows   Cuckoo-Loca

"But there's no ," says .
Sparkle-izer   Minnie

 walks in.
Daisy

"These bows belong out front," Daisy says.

"Maybe the Sparkle-izer fell into the box!"
says Millie.

20

"Let's follow  Daisy and the bows," says Melody.

21

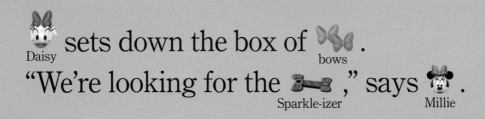 sets down the box of 🎀 .

"We're looking for the Sparkle-izer ," says Millie .

22

"I saw it on Minnie's table," says Daisy.
"It's gone!"

"Look!" says Cuckoo-Loca.
"A rubber dog bone."

"I saw  Figaro and Bella on my table," says Minnie. "Just before…"

"The Sparkle-izer disappeared!" cries Melody.

"Maybe  has the ," says .
Figaro   Sparkle-izer   Millie
"Or maybe has it!" cries .
Bella   Melody
The twins chase and .
Figaro   Bella

26

Figaro jumps into Minnie's arms.

Bella jumps into Clarabelle's arms.

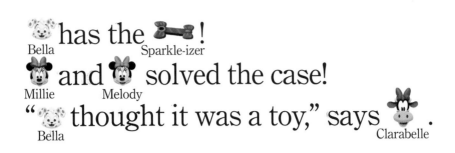 has the !
Bella   Sparkle-izer
 and solved the case!
Millie   Melody
" thought it was a toy," says .
Bella   Clarabelle

 gives  the rubber bone.
Millie   Bella

 drops the .
Bella   Sparkle-izer

 can get started.
Minnie

29

 puts  on the twins' .
Minnie   sparkles   bows
They look so cute!

 is next. He wants  on his  !
Mickey   sparkles   bow tie
The  is a big hit!
      Sparkle-izer

 thanks the twins.
"You did a sparkle-ific job!"

Minnie